UNDER THE HOOD

THE HISTORY OF PORSCHES

SETH HINGSTON

PowerKiDS press.

NEW YORK

Published in 2019 by The Rosen Publishing Group, Inc.
29 East 21st Street, New York, NY 10010

Editor: Elizabeth Krajnik
Book Design: Michael Flynn

Photo Credits: Cover (car) Grzegorz Czapski/Shutterstock.com; cover, p. 1 (emblem) r.classen/Shutterstock.com; cover, pp. 1, 3–8, 10–13, 16–20, 22–26, 28–32 (background) fotomak/Shutterstock.com; p. 5 (top) Yauhen_D/Shutterstock.com; p. 5 (bottom) Volha-Hanna Kanashyts/Shutterstock.com; p. 7 Keystone/Hulton Archive/Getty Images; p. 9 OleksSH/Shutterstock.com; p. 10 Everyonephoto Studio/Shutterstock.com; p. 11 Alexander Kirch/Shutterstock.com; p. 13 (main) Barcroft Media/Getty Images; pp. 13 (inset), 23 (main) Roman Belogorodov/Shutterstock.com; p. 14 Roger Gould/Getty Images Sport/Getty Images; p. 15 PHOTOMDP/Shutterstock.com; p. 17 (main) Oleg Golovnev/Shutterstock.com; p. 17 (inset) Igor Krapivin/Shutterstock.com; p. 18 https://commons.wikimedia.org/wiki/File:2013_Porsche_911_Carrera_4S_(991)_(9626546987).jpg; p. 19 Ivan Svyatkovsky/Shutterstock.com; p. 21 Dong liu/Shutterstock.com; p. 23 (inset) Faiz Zaki/Shutterstock.com; p. 25 Caddy Man/Shutterstock.com; p. 27 Max Earey/Shutterstock.com; pp. 28–29 blaskor/Shutterstock.com.

Cataloging-in-Publication Data

Names: Kingston, Seth.
Title: The history of Porsches / Seth Kingston.
Description: New York : PowerKids Press, 2019. | Series: Under the hood | Includes glossary and index.
Identifiers: ISBN 9781538344583 (pbk.) | ISBN 9781538343418 (library bound) | ISBN 9781538344590 (6 pack)
Subjects: LCSH: Porsche automobiles–Juvenile literature. | Porsche automobiles–History–Juvenile literature.
Classification: LCC TL215.P75 K56 2019 | DDC 629.222–dc23

Manufactured in the United States of America

CPSIA Compliance Information: Batch #CWPK19. For Further Information contact Rosen Publishing, New York, New York at 1-800-237-9932

CONTENTS

AN ICONIC BRAND

Porsche makes some of the most well-known cars ever built. The Porsche family has a rich history with cars that goes back more than 100 years! The Porsche brand is so powerful that most people can picture just what the company's cars look like.

Porsche is one of the most famous sports and luxury car manufacturers in the world. Its cars are also some of the most expensive! It's not unusual for a Porsche to cost more than $200,000. One of the reasons these cars cost so much is that they're well made, with a lot of attention paid to every detail. Even though not all Porsche models look the same, they all have common **design** elements. Porsche is known for making high-performance cars.

THE PORSCHE MACAN IS A FIVE-DOOR **CROSSOVER** SPORT-UTILITY VEHICLE (SUV). WHILE THIS CAR WAS BEING DEVELOPED, IT HAD THE CODENAME "CAJUN," WHICH STOOD FOR "CAYENNE JUNIOR." THE CAYENNE IS ANOTHER PORSCHE SUV.

PORSCHE CAYENNE S

THE PORSCHE FAMILY

In 1900, Ferdinand Porsche, an Austrian **engineer**, presented a car at that year's World's Fair in Paris, France. Porsche's first model, the Lohner-Porsche, was powered by electricity. It only went about 35 miles (56.3 km) per hour. Later, when the gas-powered engine was invented, Porsche was able to design faster cars.

On September 19, 1909, Porsche's son, Ferdinand Anton Ernst Porsche, was born. He went by the nickname "Ferry." In 1923, Porsche moved to Stuttgart, Germany, where he started a consulting company to develop racecars. In 1948, Porsche introduced its first production car—the 356. Ferry Porsche proved to have as much genius for cars as his father. After Ferdinand Porsche died in 1951, Ferry Porsche ran the company until his own death in 1998.

FERDINAND PORSCHE WAS BORN ON SEPTEMBER 3, 1875, IN MAFFERSDORF, WHICH IS A CITY IN WHAT IS NOW THE CZECH REPUBLIC.

START YOUR ENGINES

IN 1900, FERDINAND PORSCHE ALSO DEVELOPED AN ALL-WHEEL DRIVE RACECAR AND A CAR THAT RAN ON BOTH GASOLINE AND ELECTRICITY. THESE CARS ARE CALLED HYBRIDS.

SPEED MACHINES

Building racecars was something Ferdinand and Ferry Porsche loved. They knew people would pay lots of money for fast, sleek sports cars. Since Porsche's beginnings, its racecars and its sports cars have been speed machines.

In 1933, Porsche developed a Grand Prix racecar with a 16-**cylinder** engine for a company called Auto Union. The car's engine was in the back instead of the front. This idea was later used in the Volkswagen Beetle.

In 1939, Porsche developed three racing coupes, or hard-top cars. These cars, called the Type 64, were built for long-distance **endurance** competitions and are the base of all Porsche sports cars. Over the years, the Porsche company has stayed true to its sporty origins to create fast cars with light frames and powerful engines.

THE PORSCHE TYPE 64 CARS WERE MADE FROM HAND-SHAPED ALUMINUM, WHICH IS A TYPE OF METAL. THE FIRST CAR WAS DESTROYED EARLY IN WORLD WAR II, THE SECOND WAS USED BY THE PORSCHE FAMILY, AND THE THIRD WAS PUT IN STORAGE AND LATER DESTROYED BY AMERICAN SOLDIERS WHO FOUND IT.

LEFT-SIDE IGNITION

One of the things that sets Porsches apart from other sports cars is that some models have the ignition, or where you insert the key to start the car, on the left side of the steering wheel. This goes back to the placement of the ignition switch in Le Mans racecars of the past. The ignition was on the left so the drivers could start their car while they were getting into it.

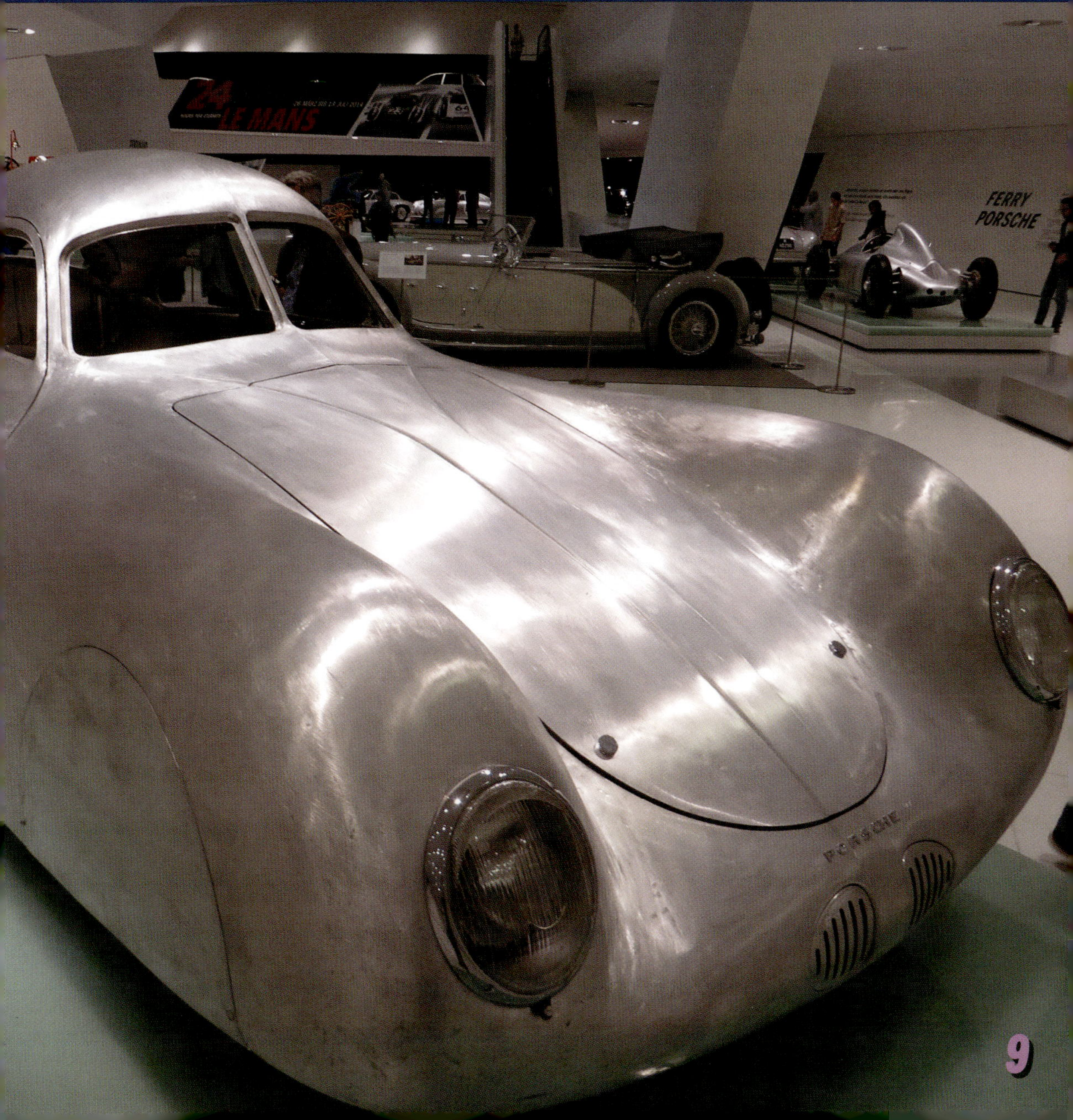

USING THE BEETLE

When Porsche began designing cars for his own company, he used the design of the Volkswagen Beetle as a starting point. Porsche started with changed and improved Volkswagen parts and the original Volkswagen design. From this, Ferry Porsche created a faster, lighter **version** of the Beetle. The new sports car, which Ferry called the 356, was released in 1948.

PORSCHE 356

THERE ARE MANY SIMILARITIES BETWEEN THE LOOK OF THE PORSCHE 356 AND THE PORSCHE 911. THESE SIMILARITIES EXIST BETWEEN MANY OF PORSCHE'S PAST AND PRESENT MODELS.

PORSCHE 911

Many people liked the 356. Not only was it more beautiful than other cars on the road, it was also much more **aerodynamic**. Porsche continued in this direction with other models. The company introduced the Porsche 911 in 1963. Once again, Ferry created the car of the future by improving upon his company's previous designs. Porsche continues to create cars as memorable

PORSCHES IN RACING

Porsche isn't just one of the most well-known sports car manufacturers. It's also one of the largest racecar manufacturers in the world. Ferdinand Porsche loved racecars. He even raced some of the models himself. Today, Porsche builds some of the fastest cars in the world. Engineers and scientists at Porsche work hard to develop new **technologies** and car designs for their high-performance cars.

The Porsche 911 became the basis for some of Porsche's most successful racecars. The company made many **variations** on the 911 to create faster cars. The 911 GT1, which was first produced in 1996, is one of the fastest cars Porsche has ever created. From 2005 to 2011, the Porsche RS Spyder made a name for itself by winning some of the biggest races in the world.

THE PORSCHE 911 GT1 DOESN'T ACTUALLY HAVE MUCH IN COMMON WITH THE PRODUCTION MODEL 911 YOU'D SEE ON THE ROAD.

START YOUR ENGINES

PORSCHE PRODUCED A LIMITED NUMBER OF A STREET-LEGAL VERSION OF THE 911 GT1 CALLED THE 911 GT1 STRASSENVERSION, WHICH MEANS "STREET VERSION" IN GERMAN.

PORSCHE 911 GT1 STRASSENVERSION

PORSCHE 911 GT1 RACECAR

THIS MCLAREN MP4/2C FORMULA ONE CAR IS POWERED BY A TAG-PORSCHE ENGINE. AS OF 2018, PORSCHE DOESN'T RACE CARS IN FORMULA ONE.

Porsche's racecars are different from its production models. Racecars are driven on special tracks, by special drivers, and have special parts and engines. Porsche's racecars also differ between styles of racing. Porsche has created racecars for different kinds of racing.

In the past, Porsche has raced in Formula One races, but it has only one World Championship Grand Prix title, which dates back to the 1962 French Grand Prix. Porsches have been successful in longer races as well. The 24 Hours of Le Mans is the oldest endurance race in the world. Cars race for 24 hours. These cars have to be fast and run for a long time without breaking down. As of 2018, Porsche has won the 24 Hours of Le Mans 19 times.

THE 911 RSR

In 2018, the Porsche model driven in the 24 Hours of Le Mans was the 911 RSR. This car has a 4.0-liter, six-cylinder engine that produces about 510 horsepower. The engine sits in front of the rear axle. The 911 RSR has a removable roof hatch so the driver can get into and out of the seat. To keep the driver safe in the event of a crash, the 911 RSR has a roll cage.

THE 356

The first car that Porsche produced to sell was the 356. It was produced in Gmünd, Austria, and nicknamed the Gmünd Roadster. The 356 was first road **certified** on June 8, 1948. It had a 1.1-liter, four-cylinder engine that produced 35 horsepower. The engine was in the rear of the car, which could reach a top speed of 83 miles (133.5 km) per hour. The 356 had rear-wheel drive.

Although the first 356 model began with Volkswagen parts, Porsche quickly improved upon the car and made it fully its own. By the 1950s, it was one of the best-regarded cars on the market. People were delighted at how easily the 356 handled. It was also faster and more well built than most other sports cars on the market.

Like most sports cars, the 356 had two doors. Later models featured convertible roofs. The fastest 356 model was the Speedster. It could reach 112 miles (180.5 km) per hour.

A NUMBER OF DIFFERENT MODELS OF THE 356 WERE PRODUCED FROM 1948 TO 1965. THE FIRST 356 WAS ONLY AVAILABLE AS A COUPE, WHILE OTHER MODELS WERE AVAILABLE AS CONVERTIBLES.

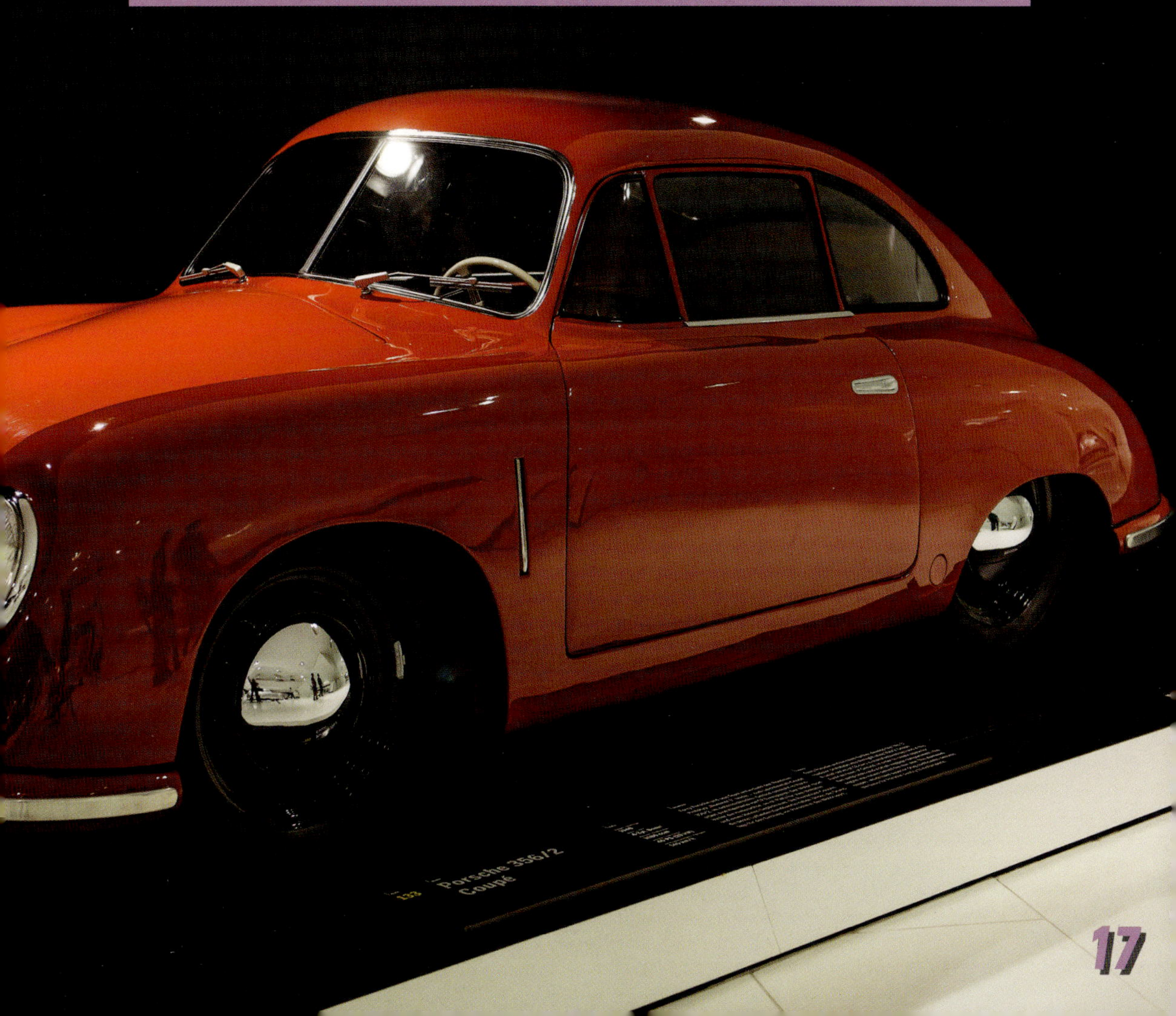
Porsche 356/2
Coupé

THE 911

The 911 was introduced in 1963 at the Internationale Automobil-Ausstellung (IAA), or the International Automobile Exhibition, in Frankfurt, Germany, to replace the 356. It was originally called the 901, but it was renamed shortly after the car went on sale in 1964. The 911 was originally only available as a coupe and had a 2.0-liter, six-cylinder engine that produced 130 horsepower.

2013 PORSCHE 911 CARRERA 4S

THE FIRST PORSCHE 911 MODEL WAS PRODUCED UNTIL 1989. THROUGHOUT THE YEARS, PORSCHE HAS PRODUCED MANY DIFFERENT MODELS OF THE 911.

START YOUR ENGINES

IN 2016, PORSCHE SOLD 32,409 CARS OF THE 911 MODEL AROUND THE WORLD. SINCE ITS INTRODUCTION IN 1963, THERE HAVE BEEN SEVEN GENERATIONS OF THE 911.

Most sports cars of the day had four speeds. The 911 had five. It was also fast! The new engine allowed it to go from 0 to 60 miles (0 to 96.6 km) per hour in just nine seconds! The 911 did more than just replace the 356. It also outsold the original car. Today, the 911 remains Porsche's best-selling model. Today's 911s, however, are faster than earlier generations of the car.

THE BOXSTER

The Porsche Boxster was launched in September 1996. This car combines performance and everyday drivability. The Boxster is a roadster, which is a car with two seats and a convertible roof. Its engine is called a "boxer" because of its shape. If you combine the words "boxer" and "roadster," you get "Boxster." The Boxster was the first Porsche sports car to be designed as a roadster since the 550 Spyder, which was produced from 1953 to 1956.

The first generation of the Boxster, called the 986, had a powerful 2.5-liter, six-cylinder engine. In 2000, the Boxster got a 2.7-liter, six-cylinder engine that produced 217 horsepower. Car buyers love the Boxster because of its classic look.

A PORSCHE 718 BOXSTER S STARTS AT $71,400 AND A BASE MODEL 718 BOXSTER STARTS AT $59,000.

THE CURRENT BOXSTER

The base model 718 Boxster can go from 0 to 60 miles (0 to 96.6 km) per hour in just 4.9 seconds and has a top track speed of 170 miles (273.6 km) per hour. Its engine produces up to 300 horsepower. The 718 Boxster S can go from 0 to 60 miles (0 to 96.6 km) per hour in 4.4 seconds and has a top track speed of 177 miles (284.9 km) per hour. Its engine produces up to 350 horsepower.

THE CAYMAN

In 2005, Porsche released the Cayman S at the IAA. The Cayman is a fastback coupe, which is a car with a roofline that slopes continuously down at the back. The car is based on the second and third generations of the Boxster. Porsche released the Cayman because roadsters aren't practical for all Porsche lovers. They have limited trunk space, and convertible roofs aren't useful for drivers who live in cold and rainy parts of the world.

The first Cayman models looked very much like the Boxster. They had the same headlights, taillights, and doors. The Cayman's most noticeable difference is its rear hatch, which allows drivers to carry bags, suitcases, and other items. The first Cayman had a 3.4-liter engine that produced 295 horsepower.

COUPES HAVE STIFFER FRAMES THAN CONVERTIBLES. THE CAYMAN S WAS 250 PERCENT STIFFER THAN THAT YEAR'S BOXSTER.

Cayman S
Porsche Cayman S Sport

THE CAYENNE

The Cayenne is Porsche's first mid-size luxury crossover SUV. Because most sports cars have only two seats, Porsche wanted to make a vehicle that would allow its customers to carry more **passengers** or more **cargo**. The Cayenne isn't as big as some SUVs, but it does have room to seat up to five people. Other Porsches had six-cylinder engines, but this bigger car needed a bigger engine. The Cayenne became the first Porsche to have an eight-cylinder, or V-8, engine since 1995. It's also the first production-model Porsche to have four doors.

In 2002, the Porsche Cayenne went on sale. This generation lasted until 2010, when Porsche revealed the second generation. The 2011 Cayenne was also available as a hybrid model.

EVEN THOUGH THE CAYENNE IS A LARGER CAR AND CAN SEAT MORE PASSENGERS, IT STILL HAS THE COMMON DESIGN ELEMENTS OF OTHER PORSCHE MODELS.

START YOUR ENGINES

THE 2004 CAYENNE HAD A 3.2-LITER, VR6 ENGINE THAT PRODUCED 247 HORSEPOWER. THE CAYENNE S HYBRID HAD A 3.0-LITER, V-6 ENGINE THAT PRODUCED 333 HORSEPOWER.

THE RS SPYDER

In 1999, Porsche retired the 911 GT1 and released a new model to continue its racing success. Named after Porsche's 550 Spyder of the 1950s, the RS Spyder was created with Penske Racing to compete in Le Mans **Prototype** Class 2 racing. It won first place in its class in its first race at the 2005 American Le Mans Series.

Porsche was back on top of the endurance racing world. Instead of using older Porsche models, engineers built a brand new V-8 engine from scratch. This engine produced a maximum of 503 horsepower. Later engines produced even more horsepower. The RS Spyder could go from 0 to 60 miles (96.6 km) per hour in about 3 seconds, and it could reach speeds of almost 200 miles (321.9 km) per hour.

THE RS SPYDER IS ONE OF PORSCHE'S MOST SUCCESSFUL PROTOTYPES. IN TOTAL, THE RS SPYDER HAD 13 OVERALL WINS AND 22 CLASS WINS. IT WON THE ALMS LMP2 CHAMPIONSHIP THREE YEARS IN A ROW DURING THE FIVE YEARS IT RACED.

THE PORSCHE 550 SPYDER

The Porsche 550 Spyder was inspired by the Porsche 356. However, it was a roadster and didn't have the hard roof the 356 had. The 550 Spyder won the first race it competed in—the Nürburgring Eifel Race in 1953. Over its racing lifetime, the 550 Spyder raced in 370 races, took home 95 victories, and won its class 75 times. Porsche only produced 90 examples of the 550 Spyder, and 43 of them were built as nonracing customer cars.

CURRENT PORSCHE MODELS

As of 2018, Porsche sells a number of different models to fit the needs of its customers. The current Boxster and Cayman generation includes the 718 Boxster, 718 Boxster S, 718 Boxster GTS, 718 Cayman, 718 Cayman S, and 718 Cayman GTS.

THE PANAMERA TURBO S E-HYBRID EXECUTIVE CAN GO FROM 0 TO 60 MILES (96.6 KM) PER HOUR IN JUST 3.3 SECONDS AND HAS A TOP TRACK SPEED OF 192 MILES (309 KM). ITS TWIN-TURBOCHARGE V-8 ENGINE CAN PRODUCE UP TO 680 COMBINED HORSEPOWER.

There are a number of 911 models that range in capabilities and prices. The 911 Carrera is available in nine different models. 911s also come in Targa 4 models, GTS models, Turbo models, GT3 models, and GT2 RS models. The most expensive 911 model is the GT2 RS, which starts at $293,200. The 911 continues to be Porsche's most loved car.

Also included in the lineup are all the different Panamera, Macan, and Cayenne models. Porsche has a model to fit the needs of almost any buyer. Which Porsche model do you like best?

TIMELINE

September 3, 1875 › Ferdinand Porsche is born in Maffersdorf, which is in the present-day Czech Republic.

1900 › Porsche presents the Lohner-Porsche electric car at the World's Fair in Paris, France.

September 19, 1909 › Ferdinand "Ferry" Anton Ernst Porsche is born.

1923 › Porsche moves to Stuttgart, Germany.

1933 › Porsche develops the Grand Prix racecar.

1939 › Porsche develops the Type 64.

June 8, 1948 › Porsche releases the 356.

1951 › Ferdinand Porsche dies.

1953 › Porsche releases the 550 Spyder.

1963 › Porsche introduces the 911 at the IAA in Frankfurt, Germany.

September 1996 › Porsche introduces the Boxster.

1998 › Ferry Porsche dies.

1999 › Porsche retires the 911 GT1.

2002 › Porsche begins selling the Cayenne.

2005 › Porsche releases the Cayman.

2005 › Porsche begins racing the RS Spyder.

GLOSSARY

aerodynamic: The qualities of an object that affect how easily it's able to move through the air.

cargo: Something that is carried from one place to another by a vehicle, boat, or airplane.

certify: To officially say that someone or something has met certain standards or requirements.

crossover: A change from one style or type of activity to another, or something that combines two or more styles or types of something.

cylinder: A tube-shaped part of an engine where power is created.

design: The way something has been made. Also, to create the plan for something.

endurance: The quality of continuing for a long time.

engineer: Someone who plans and builds machines.

passenger: Someone riding on or in a vehicle.

prototype: A first or early example that is used as a model for what comes later.

technology: The way people do something and the tools they use.

variation: A change in form, position, or condition.

version: A form of something that is different from the ones that came before it.

INDEX

WEBSITES

Due to the changing nature of Internet links, PowerKids Press has developed an online list of websites related to the subject of this book. This site is updated regularly. Please use this link to access the list: www.powerkidslinks.com/hood/porsches